TEACHER VOICE

TEACHER VOICE

Edited by DeMisty D. Bellinger
and Alan Good

Mal
arkey
Books
Denver

Teacher Voice is published by Malarkey Books and Mythic Picnic. The stories, essays, and poems contained within are published with the permission of the authors and remain the copyright of their respective authors.

Malarkey Books
PO Box 19713 Denver CO 80219
www.malarkeybooks.com
@MalarkeyBooks
@MythicPicnic

ISBN: 978-0-9981710-7-4

2019

Cover design by Stuart Buck.
@stuartmbuck

Every story, essay, and poem in this book was written by a current or former teacher and edited by two college teachers. We dedicate this book to all teachers.

TABLE OF CONTENTS

INTRODUCTION

DeMisty D. Bellinger

"LET ME USE my teacher voice." I hear this more among colleagues than anyone else, of course, being a teacher myself. For instance, someone would say it when there is no mic and, as if having a teacher's voice was a solution to a lack of artificial amplification, the person would announce that they would use their teacher voice, alleviating any fears that we won't hear their message. Teachers have the uncanny ability to be heard, to transform their normal, conversational selves to command the attention of those before us.

Teachers also can be heard over the noise of those of us who assume what it is to educate. We often know how to reach our students, be they kindergarteners or college sophomores, but our voices are often lost in political and administrative mumbo-jumbo. And we know how to articulate what it means to be a teacher—be it in the classroom or elsewhere.

When we use our teacher voice, we have something worthwhile to say. We are constantly creating lessons for our students, activities for our classes, short lectures, and discussion points. As teachers, we are storytellers and poets on our feet. Good teachers are able to build worlds. Good teachers who are writers are able to translate that on paper.

When I signed on to help with this anthology, I wondered what kind of writing would we possibly get from such a call: Assertive? Commanding? Loud and clear? Authoritarian? I was more than impressed and satisfied with the writing we received. These works are reflective, thoughtful, inviting, and entertaining. Since the only requirement was that the writer be a teacher or was a teacher in their past, the subject matter was diverse and intriguing, from an essay exploring the comfort in the consistency of fast food by James Tate Hill, to poems about the tender days of early motherhood by Chloe Yelena Miller. Of course, some of the writing is specifically about teaching, such as the absurdist short story "The New Normal" by Carman C. Curton or the isolation for people of color in academia as recounted in Wandeka Gayle's essay "The Year in Red Mountain Country."

I hope that you will find some comfort and wisdom in this collection. These pieces of writing are as varied and fascinating as the profession of teaching itself. Whether they offer insight into teaching or insight to humanity, these teachers instilled their voices and personalities in the words that follow.

WHAT I USED TO KNOW: AN ATTEMPTED SELF-REFLECTION

TOMAS MONIZ

I used to know what an essay was. And I better. I've taught basic skills writing for the last twenty years. Still do. The first day of each semester, I ask students to define in their own terms what an essay is. Because they know the answer: an intro and thesis and body paragraphs and a conclusion. I tease them: how many paragraphs, how many sentences. Five paragraphs, for sure, some student always answers with a snap. Others nod in agreement. And then I say, Correct. And then I challenge them to never write a five-paragraph essay again. And I mean it. But I'm also lying.

I used to define myself: mutt. Then hapa. Then American. Then Chicano. For years I settled on: mixed race hybrid motherfucker. Today I understand Latinx. I respect the hyphen. The contested space. I am like so many people attempting to own the privilege while embracing the fluidity.

I used to know what manhood was. As a teenager, I believed manhood was: fathers. And sports. And Saturday nights coming home late, drunk and not to be disturbed by me or my brothers. Because or else. And talking shit. But that's a lie too. Because, as I've written before, I went from teenager to father. The mother of my children never wanted me to be traditional man, but expected me to be partner and parent. Those expectations embodied the most revolutionary trust ever placed on me. Because it forced me to figure out what that meant for myself. And I failed mostly. But I tried.

One student will say, You can never start a sentence with and. Or because. Or use fragments. I nod. I say, True. Sometimes. But.

I was taught to see colonialism as a thing to study, to look back on. But to continue to believe that is to engage in acts of willful ignorance. To ignore the continuing agency and reality of colonialism within my own family as well as across the culture and institutions of this country is to position myself accomplice. Colonizer. And I am. I do. But not without resistance.

I like how Matthew Zapruder defined an essay in his book *Why Poetry*: an essay is an attempt to "engage in that hard-to-categorize effort to explore, however loosely, a certain idea."

I never knew what desire was. Or, what I mean is, I always knew my desire differed from one day to the next. Was I flawed? Suspect? I believed I was. Am. But I've learned to be more comfortable with

9

that. So today, when people ask me my orientation, I simply say: Sexual. Or if I'm feeling coy, Desiring. Or open. But maybe it's me obfuscating.

Student after student composes pieces of writing with the goal of getting an A. And of course. But more importantly, they also work at explaining who they are and what they think. In their voice. Grounded in their experience. Watching students gain fluency has shown me the necessity and relevance of writing. Of finding voice. Of speaking up and out. They inspire me that this work (the teaching and the writing) truly embodies the verb form of essay: to, with great effort, try, attempt.

Here then: That's what all this is. Attempts. Explorations. I'm trying to explain. Or rename. Or take responsibility for what I've discovered and who I am. Like we all are doing. In fact, I'd like to hear what you have discovered as well:

PO BOX 3555 Berkeley CA 94703

Good Austin, Ninja Austin

Shannon McLeod

An excerpt from Whimsy,
a novella in stories

I don't know if you ever recover from the feeling of thirty pairs of eyes all staring at you in concert, especially when they're watching you during your first day on the job. Thankfully, it's not a feeling a teacher needs to get used to. By the third day of school, you only have half of the class's attention at any given time. It's a relief once the pressure's off. By Halloween you're at the bottom of the kids' lists of interests.

In the morning, students were sizing each other up in the hallways, concerned with their decisions about whether or not

to dress up. Most of the seventh graders
hadn't worn costumes to school. They were
too "mature." But they would inevitably
beg for candy with their younger siblings
that night. A few unfortunate ones as-
sumed this year would be no different from
sixth grade—when they were in the elementary school and marched alongside the
kindergarteners in the Halloween parade. Angelo was dressed as a clown, with
full makeup, a rainbow wig, and what
must have been his dad's red Converse
sneakers. He was dragging a stuffed
dachshund behind him on a leash, chuck-
ling uneasily as his classmates laughed at
him from the sides of the hallway. The
clique of girls from the volleyball team all
wore mouse ears. I watched McKenzie
drawing whiskers on each girl's cheeks in
front of her locker. Three of them were in
my first-period English class, where I'd in-
tentionally split them up. Their assigned
seats marked three corners of the room, so
they weren't close enough to throw glances

at each other when I'd make a pop culture reference they disapproved of.

The warning bell rang and I left my hall post outside of my classroom door. I was convinced they'd given me (the newbie) this room because of the undesirable location. Here, the hallway bent, and my classroom door was set in a semi-hidden alcove, so students sought out this location for fights and make-out sessions. I had a broom by the door for when I needed to break up physical altercations of either variety.

Inside, the kids were already eating candy. Someone must have swiped a bag from their parents this morning because almost a dozen of them were gnawing on mini Snickers at their seats when the final bell rang, peanuts and crumbles of chocolate falling to their laps and onto the floor.

Austin W. sauntered in late, as usual, with his backpack slung over one shoulder. The other day, I'd heard the department chair in the teacher's lounge say, "This year they're all named Austin. I can hardly keep track of all the Austins. A few years ago they were all named Hunter. Do you remember that?" The art teacher she'd been talking to nodded with her mouth full of noodles. And she was right. There were three in my first period, alone. Austin W. was barely five feet tall. If a group of people were to approximate his age, I'd wager the average guess would be seven and a half years old. He had a baby face, baby-thin blond hair, and wore thick glasses that magnified his eyes to Disney-character proportions. The first week of school, after I'd sent him to the office four days in a row, Judith, the vice principal, told me I had to start disciplining him in class. "He's just so cute that he gets away with murder," she said. "And you need to show him he can't pull that crap."

Wasn't that her job? I thought. I was still learning.

Austin W. often talked to himself in an argumentative tone. I had a theory that he was trying to trick his classmates into thinking he had friends. Maybe he thought if he spoke aloud among groups, onlookers would think he was having a real conversation with someone nearby. A conversation where *he* was the intimidating one. Austin W. was wearing a ninja costume. One of the mouse girls made a crack about Power Rangers, and he responded by lunging his little hooded head toward her; "Beat yer ass," he mumbled. At the beginning of the year, it was alarming to witness a seven-year-old-looking child speak this way. Eventually, I learned to ignore it, like his classmates more or less had. I couldn't send him to the office for these offenses anymore. Until I figured out how to deal with them, I decided to pretend I had a hearing impairment.

I began my lesson on apostrophes. We started each day with grammar. I was looking forward to getting this mandatory chore out of the way so that I could present the Halloween-themed creative writing prompts I had prepared as a special treat. I was excited to do something fun and festive with the kids. I'd written a short story inspired by a macabre illustration I'd found on the internet. The plan was to turn the lights off and play the "Sounds of Halloween" screams track while I read the story, with the image of the old woman and her decapitated child projected on the board. After I modeled the activity for the kids, they would choose from a selection of other scary images and write their own stories.

On the board I wrote three sentences that needed apostrophes. The students copied them down. Austin W. sat at his corner seat closest to the door and karate chopped the air. In early September, I'd placed him in the front of the room. During my student teaching, my mentor advised me to put the troublemakers up front, so they would be more likely to focus on the lesson. But being at the front just meant Austin W. had the whole class as his audience behind him. And it was harder to ignore him when he was up front. Now, I'd strategically placed him with two vacant desks surrounding him: one to the side and one in front of him. He was isolated, and that was the best I could do for classroom management. The student closest to him was Austin G. (or "Good Austin," as I called him in my head), who sat kitty-corner to Austin W. Austin W. leaned over and pretended to karate-chop Good Austin's head. After a few slices of Austin W.'s hand through the air, Good Austin must have felt the slight breeze, because he swatted above him and the two slapped hands. "*Heyyy*," Good Austin whined as he swiveled around in his chair.

"Austin G., why don't you come up here and fix the first sentence on the board for me?" I said to distract from a potential hissy fit. He was always eager to show how good he was, so he walked up to the board, took the dry-erase marker from my hand, and added the apostrophes to the correct possessives and contractions. Next, I called on Liam and then Ciara.

I instructed the students to put away their grammar and get out their journals. I turned off the lights and laughed maniacally. A few students giggled.

Brody feigned a girly shriek and laughter erupted. I put on the Halloween music and turned on the projector, revealing the gruesome illustration. In the low light, I could see the whites of most of their eyes, their attention rapt. I began to read my story, in a low, creepy voice. I got that giddy feeling in my abdomen: the rare sensation I feel when my lesson is going as planned and the students are all engaged.

"He was a bad little boy," I read in my creepy voice. "Each day, he woke his grandmother from her afternoon nap with some kind of prank." I looked up from my paper and scanned the students. Good Austin was turned around again, swatting away Austin W.

"Miss Quinn, Austin isn't supposed to be wearing a hood. No hoods or hats!" Good Austin called.

I walked down the aisle of desks, reading the next paragraph, so as not to lose the attention of the other students. I kept glancing at the clock, hoping the students would have enough time to write their stories and share with partners.

"Miss *Quinnnn,*" he whined.

I did not respond to Good Austin, but I paused my reading once I reached Austin W.'s desk. I leaned down and whispered, "You need to take off your hood, Austin."

He folded his arms and turned away from me quickly, like a toddler who hasn't gotten their way.

I read another sentence. At this point, all of the students had turned around. They were more interested in my feud with Austin than the decapitation of the little boy in the story.

"You can have this back when you take off your hood." I began to slide Austin's cherished Transformers lunchbox off his desk. He grabbed it and pulled back. I sighed and let go. The class's learning was more important than this, I decided. I walked back to the board as I read the next sentence of the story, "Granny knew the way to teach the boy." I glared at Austin. I couldn't see his eyes, because his glasses reflected the light from the projector. I hoped he was looking. I hoped he could tell what I was communicating to him with my stare.

Austin W. smirked. He lifted the lunchbox from his desk. His smile widened as he threw it at me. The hard corner hit my shoulder. I heard gasps and a lone guffaw, probably Brody. I looked up at Austin, his glasses like little lasers below his polyester ninja hood. My face turned hot, my ears scalding. I reached down to pick up the lunchbox. My arm began to throw it back toward him, but my brain interfered and instead I pulled my aim to the floor. The tin lunchbox clattered against the linoleum. Chloe sped from her chair to the back of the room. She took the emergency bathroom pass off the hook on the wall on her way out the door. I watched her ponytail flop down the hallway.

I decided to keep going. There was only one paragraph left in my story, and damn it if I would let Austin W. ruin my lesson plans. I heard whispers among the students. I cleared my throat and read louder, not realizing I'd ditched my theatrical voice. I was speeding through the story now. I had reached the point where the grandmother was tying a thin metal wire across the boy's play area, soon to call him in to build blocks with her. I looked back at the image on the board, remembering to read in my shrill old lady voice. "Come here, boy! Come *play* with me!"

The light flicked on. In the doorway stood Judith, her mouth agape. Chloe cowered close behind her. The class was silent. Only to be interrupted by a shriek from the CD player on my desk.

During my planning period I walked down to the office. Judith wanted to see me. I hadn't spoken to the principal since he'd hired me, but I was becoming quite familiar with Judith. I felt the tension in my chest—which had become part of my regular state since the school year started—intensify. As I approached the main office,

I wiped my sweaty palms on my pants and opened the door. I peeked into Judith's office. She was eating fundraiser caramel corn from its plastic pail with one hand and typing an email with the other. Her desk was cluttered with decorative picture frames. They held several photos of her standing among groups of students: in the halls on "wacky hair day," in the gym at a basketball game, in front of the science center during a field trip.

Judith popped a kernel into her mouth and then held up one finger in the air. I took a seat at the small table. This was where she had her talks with students who'd been sent to her. Where I'd sent Austin W. on so many occasions.

I wondered about the likelihood that she would fire me. Maybe leave me home the rest of the week and dock my pay. I had fantasized about quitting, but I didn't really want to leave. Starting all over again would be a nightmare. If I could even find another teaching job.

My phone vibrated in my pocket. I pulled it out, instinctively, not thinking. It was Rikesh, with whom I'd had a first date a week ago, followed by radio silence. I'd been waiting for his call for days, obsessively checking my phone at two-minute intervals.

"Is that an emergency or something?" I looked up from the screen to see Judith's left eyebrow hitched, taunting me. She had spun around in her office chair. Ready to confront me.

"Uh, no." I put the phone back in my pocket.

"This is the thing about teaching." She leaned back in her chair and it squeaked. "It needs to be the most important thing in your life. Otherwise, you'll be mediocre. Anyone can be a mediocre teacher. I don't want mediocre teachers here. Mediocre teachers do damage to children's development and harm their tenuous attitude toward school." She paused to inhale, then leaned closer to me again, her breath sugary and cloying. "Middle school is the make

23

it or break it time when it comes to a child's relationship with education."

"Right, and I—"

She held her finger up again, and I closed my mouth.

"As I was saying, anyone can be a mediocre teacher. But it takes almost all your energy to be a great teacher. Because it takes up all your patience. All your commitment. If your mind, and your commitments, are elsewhere, you won't make it to year two."

That was it: a lecture. It had been enough for me, though. I left her office shaking, intent that I would do better, be better.

As I walked down the hallway, I fingered my cell phone in my pocket. I headed to the only single bathroom, which was tucked behind the band room. This was my safe space, where I'd gone to cry enough times that I could no longer count them on one hand. I locked the door behind me. The light flickered—bright, then dimmer—making the tiles appear varying shades of yellowish, then off-white at its brightest. I carefully laid toilet paper on the seat, and then sat down. I heard the brass section on the other side of the wall. The buzzing of trumpets. The awkward sliding tone of the trombones.

I looked at my phone. It really was Rikesh who'd called. I was worried I'd imagined it, or misread the screen during that quick glance in the office. He'd left a voicemail. My stomach felt like an elevator car. I remembered Judith's words, and, in an impulsive moment of self-punishment, I deleted it.

I felt what I thought was triumph. I could choose to be less selfish, to escape mediocrity.

The percussion section thundered a climbing drumroll. I placed my free hand against the tiled wall, feeling for the vibration. I imagined the instructor lifting his hands up, directing a crescendo. I pictured the students' eyes following him, all heeding his command.

I wiped my face with a damp paper towel, the scent of the recycled pulp like mulch. Lunch duty awaited me.

In the cafeteria, I stood by the trashcan, directing students to pick up the balled napkins that had missed the rim. Then a pressure bore down on my head. I reached up to feel the thin plastic rim of a witch's hat. Judith was beside me, smirking. She smoothed out the tip, lifting it straight. "Show some Halloween spirit!" She shook my shoulder. "It's for the kids."

Four Poems

Maya White-Lurie

Camilo Catrillanca

I make change in the depths of my purse
Crumbs & supermarket receipts, Histories
no anthropologist would catalogue. No
university will buy these papers
No preservations with careful notes:
She bought pasta on Tuesday.
I wonder where the point tips,
Where driving a tractor is probable cause
For Colombian jungle-trained bullets, Why I
survived a father alive
On graffiti & deleted footage.

Maya White-Lurie

First Grade Science Experiment

With wet paper towels inside labeled ziplocs,
We tended our lima beans until
Roots crept to the corners & sprouts emerged
As dancers drawing themselves on stage.

Like any good scientist, I've replicated.
In pots & plastic bottles & marmalade jars
In spotlight & shade & direct southern sun
Until decades later
My apartment is a madwoman's forest.
Peach pits crack open
Avocados dissolve in the dirt
Tomato seeds extend their spider legs,
Each a delight of discovery.

Colibrí

I can't kill ants on my desk or crickets in the garden or corner spiders, the crunch of their bodies would gain me nothing, it's too forceful to stop them from brushing their antennae one leg at a time. I've been sleeping poorly with afternoon naps while puddles dry, abandoned notebooks and chocolate potato chips and the nights sliding into mornings at their own speeds. I douse myself in other worlds, grow guilty, drown in news of tomahawk missiles and speculation. I can't stop the whirring. Can't make anything. A mother in Kentucky buys her first gun, I need new shoes, hundreds of Chileans wave signs at the pope: *Mi Paz Les Doy* and *Renuncia!* red paint on the pavement and beer-soaked Francisco hats. The bees are as good as dead. Were I any other way, I wouldn't suffer the tickle, the ants' scurrying legs across my arms, my hair their chest-high grass. I puff small breaths at them when my student steps out to fetch a drink, no harm to knock pests to the floor

but they cling to my skin, their queen
somewhere eating lemon cake. The children
bring me sugar water when I'm in their
houses, juice from which fruit they can't say,
orange or pink packets from the nanny's
last trip to the supermarket. This boy sets
two glasses around the braver ants and
though I say *no, thank you no, gracias* to
anything but water or coffee, I sip my
mouth dry and flit to the next class.

Opening the Window

A downstairs neighbor practices violin
The teacher visits every Wednesday, departs
In time for *once* with a shoulder-strap case,

Notes these days flow studiously, careful
In their pauses & repetitions, now
Golden as this afternoon hour.
Each week is less jagged with breaks,
Fewer notes jammed together in frustration.

YOUNG FRANKENSTEIN

SCOTT GARSON

Originally published in Frigg.

He has a July birthday, which will make him the youngest student in Miss Pew's kindergarten class. Too young, really. So his mother suggests.

To his father, however, Young Frankenstein is a marvel. His father will not consider holding Young Frankenstein back.

And so, on the appointed morning, Young Frankenstein stands on the porch in front of the house and poses for photos. For his age, the boy is tall. He's shy. His mother has chosen for him a pair of tan shorts and a blue-checked shirt whose crisp new collar hides his electrodes. In each of the resulting images, his black hair glistens in furrows. In some, he seems to his mother happy and proud (she posts one of these, with a heart and a caption: first day of school). But in others, he squints; he holds a weak grin. His mother feels she's peering into Young Frankenstein's tumult, his fear.

"How was my big guy's day?" she asks as they are walking home.

The hour is gusty. The boy looks hypnotized by wild nets of foliage shadow tossed on the sidewalk before them.

"Did you have a good day?" she continues. "What did you do?"

"Can we have a banana popsicle when we get home?" Young Frankenstein answers.

On the second day, as she waits for him, she looks at the drawings the teacher has mounted in the hall by the classroom door. She compares Young Frankenstein's handwriting—which is crude and highly variable, each character wide of the line— to that of the boys he's identified as his new friends, Chase and Aidan. Each of their names, as committed to paper, coheres. The boy Aidan is clearly advanced: he's been taught to form lower-case letters.

"How was your day?" she asks once more.

This time he answers immediately. "Good."

But that night, when they finish their bedtime book and lie down, he whispers to her. Aidan said, You're the monster! she learns. You're the monster! said Chase. Go away!

Her own sensible words in response to this news are a frail and distant hum.

The next morning, she waits with her son in the hall before class. She watches the parents nearby, as they talk in pairs and threes. Are they already friends? Or have they been drawn to each other by way of some evident likeness? She touches the fresh-trimmed hair at Young Frankenstein's nape. He doesn't move. When the buzzer sounds and he joins the funnel of students at the classroom door, she sees what she realizes others have seen: a child whose veins fork visibly, a boy whose eyes—so beautiful! she knows—can be lost in the shadow of his brow.

"He's too young," she sobs discreetly into her phone at her desk at work.

"He's not," says her husband. "He's doing fine."

"He's too young."

"We can't send him the wrong message," he says. "I want him to see we have confidence in him."

That afternoon, she's waiting again, trying to ease the fix of her smile, as the buzzer sounds and Miss Pew's students begin their press from the classroom. She sees Chase and Aidan. They lean, they bump one another. An easy camaraderie. She sees two girls, and now three, each in a dress, speaking, or laughing in response. She moves closer, peeks in. Young Frankenstein's classmates keep coming. As she waits, she begins to understand that she has no certain idea. She knows her son's features—his forehead and hairline, his jaw. But she isn't sure what will appear in the door. She doesn't know what she might see.

THE YEAR IN RED MOUNTAIN COUNTRY

WANDEKA GAYLE

I watched bemused from my table at the Grind Coffeehouse where I had been working on a short piece for the Commonwealth Short Story Prize. I sat there, sipping my caramel frappé with almond milk, trying to decipher what television characters the children passing through the doorway were depicting for Halloween. I counted one Buzz Lightyear, two unicorn-hybrids, one Spider-Man, one Iron Man, one Black Panther, all the while praying none of these adorable little white children passing by would be sporting a feather hat or a durag or too-dark foundation.

On that Saturday in late October, it seemed every family unit in the small town of Cedar City, Utah, had come out for the first of the season's parades along Main Street. The parents seemed as gleeful as their children and as invested in the spectacle, themselves in chiffon, spandex, and masks, their little princesses and devils hoisted on their shoulders.

I watched groups meshing and laughing and allowing their children to take candies from strangers who stood outside the businesses along Main Street holding out bowls full of chocolate, caramels, and mints to passers-by.

This projected wholesomeness was refreshing and terrifying in its persuasiveness. I had been content in my thirty-six years to remain unwed and childless. It had made relocation from Lafayette, Louisiana, to this community of 30,000 people shortly after receiving my doctorate easier than if I'd had to move a whole clan.

I had come to Cedar City to assume a yearlong visiting professorship at Southern Utah University, teaching primarily fiction as well as literature and composition to undergrads. I had found the red, rocky mountains—the snow-capped ones and the pine-covered ones jutting up from the landscape—breathtaking, and the faculty welcoming, but the insular Mormon culture was a shock to say the least. Because approximately fifty-one percent of the community is Mormon (sixty-four percent in the whole state), I noted with some annoyance that it was by design that only precious few restaurants offered a glass of wine with dinner. What was more surprising was that on occasion, several of my students, sometimes as young as eighteen, sent me excuses that they had to stay home with their sick babies or take husbands or wives to the E.R. I tried to picture myself as a married eighteen-year-old or even a twenty-something married woman and shuddered. My office in the historical Braithwaite building overlooked what was dubbed the "engagement waterfalls" where young men would kneel before their teen-aged loves and offer marriage. I noticed at least one photo-shoot of the big moment for one such couple within weeks of my employment. I stood by the window watering my ivories and shaking my head. Still I could be wrong. Who was to say they wouldn't still be married in seventy years?

I think about it sometimes, the yards of antique white fabric of my never-worn wedding dress hanging still in my sister's closet in Georgia purchased two years before that I don't think I will ever wear. My dalliance with the idea of being someone's wife then in my early thirties had been hard won but short-lived, another lifetime almost, but what struck me wasn't so much that I wanted to be a part of these laughing families waving at dancing sugar plum fairies and giant SpongeBobs coming down Main Street. I didn't. It was that I was made to feel my isolation here in a place that catered to such unions.

I don't mind being solitary until these external moments amplify it. My solitude has served me well: In it, I have produced short stories, handmade books, watercolors, piano instrumentals I am proud of. I don't count myself a shy person, but I spend long stretches of time in my office away from people, in my apartment, or on sensory solitary walks on Sundays where once the stillness used to unsettle me. It's a familiar uncomfortable feeling of being on the periphery in so many ways, not wanting to remain there but having no choice.

Earlier that week, I had walked up the stairs with a professor, a Latina who lived in my apartment building, and told her that I was struggling with these feelings of difference in ways I had never really experienced before although I had been living in America for almost nine years, but I was in Utah—black, foreign and no longer religious.

To make matters worse, I was often mistaken for a student at SUU and proceeded to tell her about it.

"I was opening the door to the education building and I held it for the student behind me," I told her, "and do you know what she said? She said it was amazing I was wearing heels to class."

That it didn't occur to her that I was the professor, perhaps because of my youthful appearance, but more so because of my dark skin, had irked me. I had looked in her face when she had made the asinine comment, and I saw the realization like a changing screen transitioning from earlier confusion to horror of finding out who I was. I just shook my head. I had worn all the markers of a professor—business casual dress, block-heeled shoes, whiteboard markers in one hand, handouts in the other—but she had been confused because the signifiers were attached to a body not often seen in positions of authority on that campus—a black female. In fact, I discovered shortly after arriving that I was the only black female professor on the campus of nearly ten thousand students, the only other black female with a PhD at the time being the Assistant to the President for Diversity and Inclusion hired at the start of that year.

"Sometimes it just gets hard. You know what I mean?" I said when we were at the top of the stairs. She nodded, her curly black hair peeking out from under a wide-brimmed hat.

She was quiet for a moment. "Your feelings are valid," she began, her Spanish accent thick and musical, "but maybe just think of yourself as unique. If your work is going well, focus on that."

I looked at her pale skin and realized the ease with which she could blend in. She gave me a warm smile, and I returned a smile I did not feel. I realized then that even there with me in the margins, she could not fully know what I meant, what I felt. Surely, she must understand my need for community, I thought, of wanting to be with people with whom one felt a kinship, with whom one could relax and be one's self completely.

I waved and walked in the opposite direction down the hall to my apartment, thinking that it was similar to how one of my white male students wrote a black main character into his short story, wanting to say something about this difference but having no real understanding of the negative tropes he had perpetuated along the way: He had written a story about a troubled African-American boy with an absentee father supposedly overseas in Iraq and a poor yet hard-working mother. This did lead to a meaningful, rousing classroom conversation about ways of successfully writing "the Other," of not making them sidekicks, or selfless and magical, or victims, or giving them exaggerated language, simply not perpetuating negative narratives we try so hard to rework into the collective American consciousness.

I could only hope this class gave a glimmer of what it takes to emphasize and replicate an experience one remains outside of.

The thing is that I have felt this isolation in Louisiana too but mainly because graduate school was isolating. Having been the only Caribbean national in the English department and one of (at the time) three black students in the English Graduate program did not help.

Plus, you never know what some Southern people really think.

My first graduate coordinator—himself a white Southern male—said this to me once a few months into my tenure when I said I would be able to get the required letters of recommendation from friendly professors I had met there. I took it to heart, wondering if it was his roundabout way of telling me he didn't think much of me either.

Their euphemisms for "I don't care for you" are legendary and laced with saccharine charm I soon came to distrust when their actions far belied their words. Note, when a Southerner says, "Bless your heart," she usually is neither offering you a blessing nor goodwill. She pities whatever perceived folly has just fallen out of your mouth.

At first, I admired the artful way that the barb is disguised until I came to a place where the politest white people lived. Utah. These are people congenial to a fault but whose politeness borders on an art form meant to hide true feelings.

An Uber driver, an elderly man I'll call Dan, to whom one day I had let slip my feelings of exclusion from the culture there in Cedar City, told me, very cheerily, that this was why there were several degrees of heaven.

"Jesus said that He is gone to prepare mansions for us," Dan said as we rode down University Boulevard. "In heaven, there are the lower rungs and the higher rungs and if you don't like what's happening here in Cedar, 'cause we live by the Scriptures here, that is why you won't be happy in the highest degree of heaven anyway."

I let it sit. I could have asked him about how this church had until as recently as the late seventies excluded blacks from the priesthood, and believed (and some may still believe) that blacks were the descendants of Cain, our black skin an indication of our evil nature, our "outer darkness." I could have asked him about the church's controversial views about the LGBTQIA+ community.

"Where does it say this about the degrees of heaven in the Bible?" I asked instead.

"Oh, it's in there somewhere in the New Testament," he said with a wave of his hand.

"Okay," I said, and looked out of the window at the red mountains, and the snowcapped ones, and the ones covered in pines.

He would later invite me to Thanksgiving with his family the following month to which I would as politely decline.

This congeniality, I feel, prevented some of my students from telling me they were displeased with me or with how a lesson went. It led them to say, "Thank you for the lesson, professor," as they left, with so much feeling that it lulled me into thinking I had met the holy grail of student bodies where everything landed squarely into their minds and they were practically salivating with gratitude. But, the anonymity of the student evaluations allowed one to write that he or she found me "cold and unresponsive," another that "felt [he] had to agree with me in order to pass the class," contrary to everything I said in class.

In fact, I have actually said the very words, "You do not have to agree with me to pass this class. You just need to prove your point."

In the other institutions where I had taught, students were far more transparent early on, so one could brace for the sourer comments.

This revelation made me wary about my students in my second and final semester, and I saw how when one student came in for a scheduled consultation, while she had been the picture of joviality at the onset of the visit, she left in a huff when I pressed her, asking her how she really felt the class was going.

"To be honest, I would much rather hear what my classmates have to say," she began. "I don't feel we get enough room to discuss our thoughts, all you do is lecture, . . . and you don't let students finish their thoughts . . . . One student was very irate when you cut her off . . . ."

I told her this was not the case. I told her that we must be existing in different realities. I remembered the odd smile but the icy blue eyes flashing hard as flint at me and realized her anger. I left that meeting with the realization that she was not miffed or frustrated, but had white, burning rage—but none of her claims warranted such feeling, I thought. It may have nothing to do with her expectations of me because of my race or my cultural difference, but it was there suspended in my mind as a possibility, or that I had unknowingly brushed up against a sensibility, a sore point, at some time in the past. She was mad for some unknown wrong that I am to this day hard-pressed to know what it was.

I polled the other students that came in for consultation that day and they did not all share her views. Still, my heart sank because I had begun to look ahead to the end of my contract with some anticipation. I would miss my colleagues who would pop by to ask if I was settling in well or to invite me to gatherings at the local watering hole or to brainstorm or to congratulate each other that we had made it to the end of the week unscathed. I just would not miss the tangled feeling teaching here gave me every day.

Certainly, I felt isolation in Michigan too but that was because I had just migrated to a tundra straight from warm Jamaica far away from anyone I knew, where some people were more straightforward in their unfriendliness.

Perhaps I have felt this way in Georgia too, even with family members across from me at the kitchen table, but it was a less tangled feeling. It was distilled of its murkiness of otherness, of being the perpetual outsider, reduced to a mere nostalgia about home, about a Jamaica we could all share. Isolation or displacement was, thereby, not as potent, nor as persistent because they were the mobile part of my Jamaica, feeding me escoveitch fish and ackee and sweet potato pudding, and playing reggae and calypso, and conversing about the grim realities of the death-tolls and corrupt politics on the island I often didn't let myself belabor.

Still, when I was in Jamaica for long periods, I found myself thinking about impending adventures, of foreign places, of new yet familiar feelings of discomfort that feed my writing.

There is an excitement too, intellectually, of being forced to face these feelings during a period of adjustment in a new place, something that is very telling about the transience of identity: You conceive of yourself differently with each new location.

In some ways we are all performing. When I wear my Dashiki and go into Lin's Market and five white strangers come up to me before the end of the fifteen-minute grocery run to say that they like my dress, they are performing an act of acceptance they feel they must actually articulate. I am performing my ideas of my Afrocentric identity and even when it becomes exhausting to field these comments about my dress, about the beads I wear, about the prints I wrap myself in, about the coily texture of my natural hair and all the extensions I wear, I understand I am a transplant in a place that does not see these markers of difference often. I cannot

51

blame them for feeling compelled to inter-
act with it. Whether they know it or not, I
feel they are giving into an unconscious
need to reassure me that my difference is
somehow not objectionable to them, albeit
unsolicited.

Once, I saw members of the fundamen-
talist sects of The Church of Jesus Christ
of Latter-day Saints in Smith's supermarket, that brand of Mormons who live on
compounds, whose women wear their hair
in fish-tails and updos and whose ankles
and elbows and clavicles are always covered in long buttoned-up A-line dresses in
solid colors. I looked at them in disbelief
because I had only seen them in documen-
taries, their stories often told from per-
spectives other than their own. I instinctively pulled out my camera phone ready
to snap away as though I had come across
a rare creature in a clearing. I would post
it to my Facebook wall to show online
friends who had joked that I better not get
married off to a Jethro or a Zebedia while I
was in Mormon country.

Then I froze. I realized in that moment that I was doing the same thing that had been done to me much of the time I entered a white space. I was perpetuating the othering to this subset of white people, themselves on the periphery of society because of their supposed fanaticism. I lowered my camera and put it back in my bag.

Sure, they could blend into society if they so chose by changing their signature clothing and hairstyles while I cannot change my skin. We aren't exactly the same, but I realized in that moment that I didn't want to make anyone feel the exclusion I felt on a daily basis being in this body and living in this place.

The landscape in Utah made me feel simultaneously solitary and insignificant but, in a way, put my problems in context. The light is different in Utah. "Bright," is how a fellow new faculty member called it. The landscape feels open to the sun, splayed out like a spread-eagled palm, succumbing, vulnerable. We see the whole sky here. The landscape recedes to it and like this landscape, I felt hyper-visible. I had to once again face feelings of separation it brought.

I am not a natural hiker. In fact, if I can admire all of the outdoors from my perch by an open window, I would be hard-pressed to leave my apartment, but when I traveled the trail at Capitol Reef with a group of faculty members after a writing retreat in Loa, I looked at the intricate spirals and formations and the vastness of these towering red rocks. It made me remember my smallness, how massive the world is, how easily it may swallow up our problems, just for a moment. It was exhilarating and humbling and is one thing I think I will miss about my time here.

I feel I have lived at least two lives since I've been here even more than in any other place—a public life and a private one. In public, I have had to maintain my composure even through all the micro-aggressions; I can't show I'm upset by what a student may have said about me in secret; I can't break down when I miss my family or when a wave of melancholia

washes through me; I can't become the ste-
reotypical angry black woman for any reason whatsoever.

Repress. *Breathe*. Repress. *Breathe*.

In private, I let myself fall to pieces; I
text a close friend who lives in New Orle-
ans. I call my oldest friend who lives Canada and she makes me laugh. I call my
mother and my father and my siblings. I
watch *King of the Hill* reruns while I create mini books for my online shop. I write
and write and write in my handmade journals until I have drained these negative
feelings like a bloodletting. I give my pro-
tagonists these feelings.

Write. *Breathe*. Write. *Breathe*.

In my first semester, I went to a get-
together dubbed the Women of Color circle,
a few women employed at SUU from all
over—Palestine, Nepal, Virginia, the Phil-
ippines, Hawaii—who sought out each other to connect each month over humus and
rice and peas and cider and heart-to-
hearts. This is what I wanted when I had
told the Latina tenant about my feelings of
exclusion. Commiseration. Celebration.

Community. Something I'm sure she'd appreciate. They still meet once a month.

On my way out of the student center in my second semester, I ran into a black student who had welcomed me my first day on campus. She raced over and hugged me.

"I'm graduating this year," she said, beaming. "It's just sad you won't be with us, but I understand. I heard about the new job in Atlanta."

We shared bemused smiles, the unsaid clear to us both.

"It actually has been an interesting experience here," I said. "I'm just sorry I wasn't as involved with the BSU's activities in my first semester."

"Oh we loved your presentation at the Step Show and the Black History Month lecture this semester," she said. "Plus, remember we want to give you an award at the black excellence ball next month."

"Oh, that's really sweet, and I am looking forward to getting all dressed up," I said, smiling. Then sobering, "I just feel like there was more I could have done from the beginning especially being the only black professor here. The thing was that I was so depressed for most of the time last semester," I said.

I didn't plan to share that, but there it was. She looked at me, eyebrows raised.

"Yes. For three or so months, I was just depressed." I couldn't stop myself.

"Now I feel a lot more settled in myself, but now my time here is ending," I said.

"We do meet every Wednesday at six," she said. "Maybe you want to come by and talk to a few students about how to stay focused. Some of them are a little lost here, you know?"

I nodded.

"Wednesday sounds good," I said. "I can definitely plan a little talk."

I am not a hugger, but this time, I hugged her as we parted.

"I'll do what I can," I said.

As I walked away, feeling fatigued by my own guilt, I felt hopeful too. I was sorry I had spent months wrapped up in my own melancholia, that I had not seen how they had needed me, that I had been outside of

the BSU in ways I felt outside of that waving crowd along Main Street during that
Halloween parade months before.

At least there's still a little time, I
thought with renewed purpose as I opened
the doors and followed the path leading
back to my office.

FOUR POEMS

NOAH CAIN

spring recess

snow melts
storm names puddles after northern lakes
canthook, badwater, nipigon
pretends she's fishing
pretends she's a fish
change of clothes
plastic bagged in the office

mister s watches
storm long out the window
dictionary open, corrective
grip pencil in hand—allowed
outside once the definition
of "consequences" is written
in full

the bell rings
bring it here
chaos covers the foolscap
scribbled tornados, bolts
of lightning, flames
he crumples the paper
why?
storm looks at her feet
no—I want you to tell me why

at fifty, midweek vacation from thunder bay
(previously published in *The Walleye*)

a jeep man steers with his knees, pours
a small tim's into
a robin's travel mug
few glugs of baileys
from the bottle under his seat
faded tan prowler, faded orange stripe
in tow—twelve footer
on the roof rack he welded himself

beads of condensation cling
to the old vienna bottle
in his right hand, scans
the wrong side
of a nameless nolalu road
for the turnoff to canthook lake

white tail on a pink jig
three picks on a stringer

cleanses himself with water
from an upturned home

depot bucket after he sweats
in his makeshift plywood sauna

glowing in the smoulder
of a pallet fire
long way from the rink
(and anything at all) moon rising
smell of deet, belly full
of fish and old vienna
the top prospect
tries not to blame
the man
who raised him
for how he did it

   your mother
   was a real looker
   dad said tail end
   of a bender

cracking the blue cap
off another

trepanning

(Previously published in *Contemporary Verse 2*)

three point mayfield® infinity skull clamp
system
high whine medical grade
reciprocating saw
a keyhole is cut
into the density
of your parietal bone
to take the pressure off
your brain

rocky point, pink glow badwater
lake sunset, circle bone amulet
cordgrass chain, you draw a bullseye
on a log-face with a calid
piece of charcoal, the rings
your tracer

I know
you can't feel my hand
on your surprisingly warm
shoulder but I touch you
anyway

red eye

his right hand
a skin and blood satellite image
of northwestern ontario
in a highwater
year

two a.m.
eats leftovers
the metallic scrub

of mom cleaning up
steel wool on still warm
cast iron

he echoes alcohol and brut
wobbles, slides his plate
on the counter

kisses her cheek
as he snores on the floral couch
she offers him
a yellow ice cream pail
receives an empty bag

of milk, a thawing pork chop
he had been holding
to his eye—

she'll fix it for him
when he wakes up
with some eggs
rye toast unbuttered
a glass of equal parts
beer and tomato juice
the way his father took it

EIGHT TIPS FOR LIVING WITH THE MONSTER UNDER YOUR BED

DEREK HECKMAN

Originally published in Wigleaf.

1. Climb onto the kitchen counter to take the salt from the highest shelf. Pour a perimeter around your bed, then look at it and pour a second perimeter a little further out. Pour a third. Turn the lights off one by one: The ceiling light, the light in your closet, the lamp on your bedside table. Set an alarm so that you wake up an hour before your mother. In the morning, hold your breath as you kneel with the broom and dustpan. Don't think about how the first two lines look like someone scraped them over with a rake. Don't think about

how the third line, too, now juts in wavy
points, like something from inside of it was
pushing with a testing finger. Just sweep
the salt up carefully and flush every grain
down the toilet.

2. Don't tell your mom. Don't tell your dad.
Don't tell your best friend Tyler, or your
other best friend Mike. Don't tell Megan
the babysitter, or Mr. Anderson your soc-
cer coach. Don't tell your teacher. Don't tell
your doctor. Don't tell the parents who
drive in your carpool. You are eight now,
too old to believe in monsters, even if, by
this point, it has learned how to say your
name; even if, by this point, you've learned
how to say its name, too.

3. During the day, attempt an offering.
Make a note of what works and what
doesn't. Peanut butter sandwiches. Carrot
sticks. Fried chicken. M&Ms. If the monster likes something, you will know, because in the morning the food will be gone.
If the monster likes something, you will

know, because you will have slept through the night. Keep good track. The monster is fickle and something that works on one night might not work on the next. Keep trying. Texas sheet cake. Orange peels. Spaghetti. If the monster doesn't like something, you will know this as well.

4. Your brother didn't have a monster. Your brother had an angel. He said that it was beautiful. He said that it scared him to death. He said that it looked like lightning entering a black hole. He said that it looked like wind whipping through a mountain forest. He said that when it spoke to him, it spoke in his own voice, amplified through a speaker the size of the storm on Jupiter, and always in a language he couldn't understand. He said and he said and he said and he said, and because of all that saying, your parents sent him away. Not saying requires practice, then, because saying is in your blood. Write everything down and burn up the paper. Go down to the lake in the woods

behind your house and scream it across the water. Stare into the bathroom mirror and see how long you can hold a smile. Don't let it droop by a centimeter, and mark the time on your brother's old stopwatch.

5. At the dock on the lake in the woods behind your house is a rowboat that's been tied there forever. The rope that keeps it moored in place is thick and the color of termites. When you pull your hands away from it they smell like rocks and old rain. Scatter pebbles on the floor of the boat and lie down in it and take a nap. In this way you will learn to sleep on a surface that is hard and rough, on a bed that's constantly rocking with the movement of something huge.

6. Offer it paperclips. Offer it coins. Offer rocks and sticks and the bones of small creatures you find along the shore of the lake. Offer the dregs of your dad's coffee. Offer the lipstick your mom throws away. Offer it the failed history test Megan the

babysitter leaves on the sofa. When, for
periods of time, it doesn't seem to like anything, offer it absolutely nothing for a
while, and see how it likes that.

7. You will want to say it by drawing. You
will want people to see. You will make
great loops for tentacles. You will draw
huge curves for claws. You'll make groups
of tiny circles with dots in them for eyes,
and draw great jagged slashes for wings.
Stop it. Remember how you're trying not to
be a person who says and use a grip of
brighter colors to transform the picture in
front you. Turn tentacles into roller coast-
ers, claws into snowy hills. The eyes could
be anything from frog eggs to sushi rolls,
and upside down, the wings could be
mountains. Your teacher will praise your
imaginative art. At night, slide the pic-
tures under your bed. Listen to the noises
the monster makes, how it seems, almost,
to be laughing.

8. Sometimes the monster will be too much.
Sometimes your salt defenses will fail and
your offerings of food and other items will
seem to send it into a rage. Don't try to be
a hero then. Just get up and go. Leap over
the salt and hurry to the door. Open it and
shut it without looking back. You cannot
go to your parents' room. You're too old
now to crawl into their bed. You'd like to
talk to your brother about it, but the num-
ber for where he is isn't anywhere in the
house. Go into his room, but don't turn on
the lights. Don't look at anything except
the dark shape of his bed. Get on the floor
and crawl under it. Swipe the dust bunnies
out of your way. Reach your fingers for the
angel and feel it there, reaching back. Curl
into a chest that hums like a giant beehive.
Feel on top of your head breathing as hot
as a bear's. Within the cosmic thunder of
noises exploding here beneath the box
spring, hear what sounds like weeping.
Hear a wave bringing a mountain low.
Hear two words over and over again, loud
as a planet: I know, I know.

THE NEW NORMAL

CARMAN C. CURTON

"It is not the purpose of this committee to place blame," The Reverend Walther Browning explained in the face of the student's tears, "but a pregnancy on campus is a clear violation of our code of conduct. Assault or not, consent or no, your expulsion is official and final."

Seven hearings later, though, the devout men of the Frontier Baptist College Morality Committee agreed: something had to be done. Women rarely earned the plentiful athletic scholarships and so generally paid full tuition. Another semester or two and they'd have no female students left.

When the chancellor's daughter gave unexpected birth right in the middle of chapel, minds were made up. "Henceforth," the trustees declared, "no female student will be without a male escort on campus. A man will sleep in every room. SROs— Sexual Resource Officers—will be posted in all women's bathrooms as well as in the women's locker room. After all, the only defense against a bad guy with a penis is a good guy with a penis."

Following a precipitous drop in enrollments the next semester, the Morality Committee stopped suspending pregnant students.

"We can't keep men out of every room," declared the president. "Frontier Baptist is different. It's right there in our name, the need to explore the boundaries of the unknown. And what's more unknown than a woman?"

That semester the college opened a daycare on campus. "There's no stopping this process now," decried the dean. "We've got too many penises out there to control them."

Within months the daycare center was filled beyond capacity.

"Penis Comitatus empowers me to deputize all men in the county over the age of 15," declared the chief of campus security. "We must defend the morality of women against assault from those rare individuals who will abuse their right to have a penis."

The following semester, the Code of Conduct was quietly changed to allow breastfeeding and diaper changes in all offices and classrooms.

"A penis-free zone just means let's go in there and let's use our penises. That's no protection at all," asserted the campus medical director.

At Spring Commencement, the president reached out to shake the hand of a graduate and accidently squashed the full diaper of the baby she held on her hip. The diaper erupted, pushing several gelatinous lumps out and onto the president's velvet robes. Backing up and shaking his arm in horror, he tumbled off the stage, breaking his pelvis, right fibula, and two ribs. Bending over to aid him, the dean got a whiff of the putrid mess and turned away politely to vomit on the elegant pyramid of remaining diplomas. Nobody noticed the tiny particles dripping from the ceremonial cap of the registrar, who brushed the celebratory cake with his gold-and-green tassel while cutting it at the reception that followed. By the next morning, half the campus had what a press release referred to as "severe intestinal distress."

"Declaring Frontier Baptist an open penis campus is really the only solution," the director of public relations said on Local 4 News the following Monday. "All men will participate in open carry, their penis out and proud at all times, or risk demerits."

He looked gravely into the camera.

"This is the new normal," he said. "We hope you will all hold us in your thoughts and prayers."

EVERYTHING YOU'VE NEVER TASTED IN TACO BELL

JAMES TATE HILL

Originally published in
The Museum of Americana

The summer you lose much of your eyesight, Taco Bell introduces its first new sauce in your lifetime. You are sixteen, and growing blind spots in the center of your left eye have spread to the right. By the time doctors diagnose your untreatable condition, you've tried the so-called Wild Sauce, but it's disappointing: a blend of burnt tomato and excessive heat. Rather than enhancing the other flavors, a dissonant sourness is all you taste. Soon Taco Bell removes Wild Sauce from the menu, and you return to high school, legally blind,

unable to read or drive but with enough
peripheral vision to sometimes pass for the
sighted teenager you used to be. In your
hometown, progress has always been
measured by the arrival of chain restaurants. The 1980s saw the first Bennigan's
and Domino's, the 1990s Applebee's, Out-
back, and Olive Garden. You are proud to
say, however, that you have never lived in
a world without Taco Bell. Long after
Charleston, West Virginia's, first "authen-
tic" Mexican restaurant opened downtown,
and despite the many meals and sombrero-
clad birthdays you celebrated at Chi-Chi's,
Taco Bell remains your favorite Mexican
food. Some friends dispute your classifica-
tion of Taco Bell as Mexican food, but what
else do you call a menu featuring tacos,
burritos, nachos, and—note the adjective
in this last item—Mexican Pizza? What
you eat says a lot about your personality,
and your love of ethnic cuisine like Taco
Bell reveals an adventurous spirit. While
elementary schoolmates clung to burgers
and fries, you were experimenting with

Taco Bell's little-known green sauce, taken off the menu the previous decade, but your parents knew they still offered it upon request. In college you meet people who regard Taco Bell as somehow inferior. Their opinions of other fast-food chains are rarely more charitable, but you can't help but take it personally each time someone spins an urban legend of cockroach eggs from the ground beef hatching in the intestines of Taco Bell customers. Your affinity for Taco Bell exudes none of the worldliness you thought it would with new friends from larger cities and states more populous than West Virginia. You don't mention that, unlike the college's cafeteria, at Taco Bell and other fast-food restaurants, you don't need anyone to read you the menu. What they have never changes. By way of a rejoinder to ad hominem attacks on your beloved Taco Bell, you tell a girlfriend about the summer before your eyes got bad, when your family watched the world's top tennis players compete in a tournament in Cincinnati. Returning to your Holiday Inn after a night match, you crossed the high-way to a Taco Bell whose employees informed you they were closed. The door was unlocked, they said, because "that tennis player, Andre Agassi, knocked on the door and we let him order." Weeks removed from his first Grand Slam championship at Wimbledon, Agassi was such a fan of the chain, you heard somewhere, that he had a makeshift Taco Bell on his private plane. For years, this is one of the stories you tell to validate your taste and identity. And if a story about tennis helps people forget you can no longer play tennis, watch tennis, or cross a highway, so be it. It's a myth that the other senses of the blind are enhanced or superior to those of the sighted. Without vision, or in your case very much of it, the visually impaired merely pay more attention to sounds, smells, tastes, and sensations. Whether or not Taco Bell is in fact the embodiment of the risk-taking, wind-mill-chasing lifestyle you thought it was, eating the same, familiar foods might not be the most expansive use of your senses.

The subtleties of Picasso's Blue Period will always elude your limited acuity, but can't you compensate with a more sophisticated palate? An ear for jazz? You'd love to name a perfume a girl is wearing, like Al Pacino in Scent of a Woman, but you don't know that many girls. In graduate school, more cultured friends introduce you to Thai food, Vietnamese, Indian, eventually and not without significant consternation, sushi—not California rolls, but the kind with actual raw fish. Noting the wide gap between coffeehouse coffee and the Folger's you make at home, you learn about grinding your own beans, French presses, the different flavor profiles from Africa, Central and South America, islands in the Pacific. In short order, you're able to locate hints of lemon and lavender in a cup of Honduras, vanilla and caramel in Nicaragua, honey and black tea and champagne in Ethiopia Yirgacheffe. After years of Pasta Roni and Dinty Moore beef stew, you begin to cook. Really cook. Risotto and pesto, tuna steaks and Parmesan-crusted chicken breasts,

81

enchiladas and chilaquiles—real Mexican food. Chopping vegetables without seeing them isn't difficult. It was laziness and inertia, it seems, and not blindness that kept you out of the kitchen. The cooking, of course, is for a girl. Something always is. Your practice of downplaying your disability while getting to know someone often gives the wrong impression of what you can and cannot do. The wrong impression is the one you prefer, even if it hasn't served you particularly well. Your new girlfriend's reactions when you're unable to join her for a subtitled film, get much out of an art museum, or find her in a crowd seem to vindicate your lies of omission. You move in together and to compensate for your limitations, you resolve to do all the cooking and the cleaning. For five years, it is enough. Except, two months after the wedding, she tells you she has made a mistake. She needs someone who can not only cook, but locate ingredients in the grocery store, drive there, and obtain them. "Your world is so small," she says, but to you it feels enormous, a gigantic mystery you will never solve. Your best friend flies to Nashville to drive you back to North Carolina. While you load the moving truck, your wife offers to grab lunch from a drive-thru. She asks what you want, and you think about it. "Taco Bell." In time, you will go on dinner dates with other women: truffle fries with garlic-lime aioli, duck confit in a cranberry reduction, crab quesadillas dipped in egg yolk. You will learn that the foods you share with dates matter less than what you tell them. Today, however, your wife and best friend make small talk while you chew your Double Decker Taco. For the first time, completely and with every taste bud, you understand why they call it comfort food. You couldn't be more grateful for how familiar it tastes: the balanced tang of red sauce, the crunch of shell after the give of flour tortilla, the lettuce just a little salty from the seasoned beef. It tastes like the best days of your life.

Four Poems

Chloe Yelena Miller

Sleep

four months old

I hear your animal cries—
they breach a night-fog of exhaustion.

I reach for your hand under my back
to pull your sixteen-pound body out from
under me.
Lit by the city street lamp,
I see you, blue,
hair rubbed thin on the side
where you struggled.

These are the nightmares of parenthood.

I lift you out of your crib,
carry you to the window.
No longer crying,
your breath still broken
by an occasional, leftover cry-gasp.

A raccoon scurries on the thin, high
branches. His eyes catch
the neighbor's backyard security light.
Maybe you can't see that far yet,
especially before the light of dawn.
I'm afraid the raccoon might fall.

You sleep in my arms—
mouth alternating
between sucking, smiling on just one side,
sucking again. Sometimes another gasp.

I don't dare sleep.

Uniquely Human

almost nine months old

*The curve of your lower back absorbs shock
when you walk. It is uniquely human. –
Smithsonian Museum's Human Origins
Program*

I bend my knee to thrust my hip,
coined-scarf chimes.
Soft body that held you, almost pushed you
out,
mimics the instructor in the dance studio
mirror.

Three weeks early,
you now have been in the dry world
longer than you lengthened in my womb.

Clapping hands against the kitchen floor,
you crawl, lift your bottom:
upright ready.
Your father and I model walking,
hold you in front of the mirror.

You wobble, almost dance in your crib,
fingers wound around the wooden slats.
Your mouth opens to scream, then smile,
then scream.

My bones, from hips to feet, spread with
your growth
and I navigate this new body.

Heat

Morning bird-songs startle you awake,
legs stretch out.

You walk stiffly through the grass, never
bending knees;
heat wriggles behind ears, knees.
You bend your neck toward the newest
sprouts.

Summer night sky stalls;
we read two more animal-sleep books.
You turn the pages, forward and back-
ward, create a new narrative.
Your baby-song crescendos before you gain
sleep-weight.
Back against my stomach,
you pull my hand around your waist to
grasp my finger.

You were an amphibian
before the anticipated dry-earth breath,
then an unfurled fawn in the crib.
Your animal cries cracked the paint,
and now you aim your body with purpose.

I must let go so you can sleep, so I can
sleep,
but I wait, breathe your escaping heat.

Pregnancy

Collage from popular pregnancy books

Beat the clock!
Get on the expectant express faster.
Wondering when your eggs will be ripe?
There's nothing you can do about your
age.

Eat healthy!
Oysters may also hop up your fertility
while raising the libido roof.
Have the male partner drink something
caffeinated
an hour before sex (to speed up his boy-
making boys.)

Once you've overcome fertility problems
and become pregnant (congratulations!),
you face a somewhat greater chance
of other problems . . .

The Key Bearer's Parents

Siân Griffiths

*Originally published in
American Short Fiction*

We were good parents. We know people assume otherwise when they see our wide ties and honking red noses, but we were. We took that job seriously. We told our son that he could be anything he wanted to be, just like you're supposed to. Yes, we could see his embarrassment when we showed up for Career Day, how he threw the basketball into the field as our tiny car pulled in so that his friends would look away. And though we were happy clowns, smiles broader and wider than any lips, the disappointment underneath our makeup was easy to read. "It's fine," we said, fitting on our over-sized shoes and adjusting the flowers in our hats. We told ourselves that he would get over it.

On the news, the talk was all nuclear war and how to avoid it. The broadcasts filled with the whole "key bearer" plan. Ethicists argued that war would be less likely if some kind of key were implanted in a person's heart. What president wouldn't pause if he had to stab the bearer to drop that bomb? The president, they said, must be the first to bloody his hands.

We sheltered our boy from all of that talk. Children should have aspirations. They should believe in their own future, if nothing else. We gave him tennis lessons, enrolled him in Spanish and pottery classes. No sooner did he tell us what his friends had signed up for then we were in the Parks office, signing him up as well. Sure, we showed him our own trade secrets—how to walk in hoop-belted trousers, how to paint a face that reduces you to a single emotion—but he wasn't really interested, and we wouldn't hold him back. We only wished his aspirations weren't so heavily laced with judgment against our own.

Fine, though, fine. While Congress continued its endless debates, we sent him to prep school and on to private college, exhausting all that we'd saved, then a series of loans. Even early on, we worried over his talk of graduate school, an MBA, and how on earth we would afford it. He wanted to be a professional, he said.

"A professional what?" we never asked. He'd decide that in time. We pictured him leaning over a mahogany desk, sleeves rolled and tie abandoned, late at the night when everyone else in the office had left. We pictured his boss patting him on the back one morning and telling him he'd made partner or would be the new CFO or had earned whatever accolades his future business would hold.

The summer before his junior year, our son came home, played tennis with his friends in the morning and drank bourbon in the afternoon. No one should be so angry wearing white shorts. In Congress, the idea of burying the key to nuclear annihilation, like treasure in a human chest, was gaining traction. "What about a trip to the fair?" we asked. "We'll get elephant ears, ride rides. You always loved the tilt-a-whirl."

"Fuck the tilted world," he growled, impressed with his own cleverness and word play, as he once again grabbed his racquet and headed out. Makeup-less and un-costumed, we watched him play, relegated to the parked car where we were something separate. He scowled through the chain link, each serve fueled by rage. His forehands brutal, his overheads unapologetically smashed into the stomachs of his opponents.

"Perhaps he'll be a tennis coach?" we whispered. That at least would bring some kind of joy, right? A brand of entertainment?

When he decided not to go back to school, there was the electrician apprenticeship, and we thought, ok, no college, no being a professional, but blue collar is fine.

Our last electrician complained that he could only charge $58 an hour here when he got $92 in California ten years ago—all of which seemed hopeful enough. It was more than we'd ever seen clowning, but that's life in the arts for you. Our boy was practical. Maybe he'd had too much time with his snobby friends? Now, if he wanted, he didn't have to play tennis any more or talk to anyone who did. We thought maybe his anger had spent itself out.

When the bill passed, even the electrician thing evaporated. Yes, they voted, a bipartisan victory, and called for a volunteer to fill the key bearer's post. Good benefits, they claimed, a life of luxury, so long as you were willing to be murdered at any moment.

We snorted at the nightly news. "Who," we said to one another, "would ever volunteer for such a thing?" The whims of politics, the fickle world? Be serious. Life was too precious. If we knew anything, we knew that.

Our son was already filling out the online application. And now that he's been selected, fished from their pool of thousands of applicants, we know we should be happy for him. He has what he wanted: steady pay, gourmet food on demand, a home in the nation's mansion, all the time in the world for tennis.

Still we can't help wondering: Is it easier to kill a man who never laughs? This boy of ours... We wish we could paint a smile on his face, teach him to spread cheer. We wonder how he ever grew so joyless. We tried to show him better, right to the end. "Money," we said, "is the root of all evil." He only looked at us, mustering the closest thing to a grin he's ever possessed. "Yes," he said, "but a man needs roots."

Note from the author:

I owe debts of inspiration to the *Barrelhouse* "Stupid Idea Junk Drawer" for the writing prompt "clown parents disappointed in non-clown child" and to the Book Fight! podcast. In an episode devoted to writing prompts, Tom had found a prompt that suggested writing a story that ended with the line "Money is the root of all evil, and a man needs roots." As he and Mike discussed how ridiculous and unhelpful a prompt it was, I couldn't help but agree and decided I'd better take it as a challenge. Wanting to up the ante for what was now a kind of "found fiction" and create an homage to a podcast I love, I gave myself the additional challenge to weave in two favorite lines from recent episodes: "A professional what?" and "No one should be so angry wearing white shorts." Thank you, Mike Ingram and Tom McAllister, for your weekly dose of intelligence, wit, and word play.

THREE POEMS

CLARENCE BARBEE

New Millennium Credit Recovery Teacher

She left me
little origami birds
from all the
quiz checks
I gave her.
There was
mutual appreciation
experienced.

Other Side of the Desk

We
were
told to
shut it down,
in the
back of the class.
Referred to as the
back of the bus.

All Black.
Faces
gravity ridden
till
wrinkled with frustration
and
knuckles paled with anger.
He
knew
no better
was/is/will never be
an excuse.

White voice.

Confused as
quivering eyes met
frustrated brown faces;
escorted out to empty hall
via
conscious, calm Black student.

Terminology discussed.
Apologies given.

Today
the voice
learned from
the face;
acceptance occurred,
and
lessons learned.

Clarence Barbee

The Love of This, Looks Past This

Tired.
The word that
most comes to mind
after tackling issues of
entitlement, ineptness, and apathy
all day.
Put your phones away.
Pay attention.
Listen!!

That text can wait,
no need for a current
status update.
Boy/girl/them/they
can you make a
better attempt to
arrive on time?

Where is your pass?
What's that smell?
Can someone please open a window?

Go get security.
Just because it's legal in the city,
don't mean
it's sanctioned
in this school—
Oh that means approved, accepted,
authorized—sanctioned. S-a-n-c-t-i-o-n-e-d.
Sanctioned.

And then we
repeat, repeat, repeat.
Like broken records
till expectations are
recorded in the DNA
of their memory cells.
And they can walk in quiet,
sit down respectfully,
pull out their own pen and paper,
give their full attention to the front of the
room,
and get ready to learn.

BREAKFAST WITH THE YOUNG PROFESSIONALS

Jonathan Persinger

In a hotel ballroom where dozens of well-dressed forty-somethings hobnob and enjoy a breakfast buffet, I am a twenty-four-year-old unable to eat a single piece of cantaloupe. I can't bring the fruit to my mouth. I can do no more than push it around my plate, because Stephen, my friend, my Director of Research, is absent, and I am a young professional.

My fork pushes the cantaloupe one more time. My eyes remain locked on the entrance, through which drip old men in suits and old men in suspenders and old women in pastels. They smile upon recognizing friends or coworkers or the smell of bacon. I despair.

When Steve does lurch through the doorway, young and frizzy-haired and wiry and a moron, wearing a blue blazer and khaki pants and looking like a hipster boat captain, I experience a moment of peace.

Steve stumbles on his way toward the tables of breakfast delights. He smiles too wide at everyone he passes and keeps nodding his head in a way reminiscent of a horse. He stands over a tiny grill, examines its contents, then picks up a piece of bacon by hand and bites the strip in half.

My moment of peace passes.

I forget about the cantaloupe, bolt upright from my seat, and start my long march across the ballroom. Reaching Steve before he commits any act more unsavory than failing to use proper silverware is imperative.

Halfway to my destination, Marie appears in front of me. Marie, Vice President of the organization, a stout woman who, this morning, looks like an orange.

"Mich*ael*," she says with her questionable emphasis, "have you seen *St*even?"

I have yet to take my eyes from him. "Yes," I tell her. "I already touched base with him. He's fantastic. His speech will be fantastic. I promise you, all the things happening today will be fantastic."

Marie replies, "I forgot to get coffee," and scampers off to rectify her problem as I scamper off to rectify mine.

I stand next to Steve, who now stares, contemplating, at a pitcher of orange juice.

He says, "How much pulp do you think is in this, because to me, pulp is *important*." I smell the vodka on his breath. My suspicions have been confirmed. Disaster is imminent.

With a smile I tell him, "We're going upstairs."

Steve says, "But I want to eat muffins."

With a smile I tell him, "We're going upstairs."

Steve says, "But I want to yell at Marie."

I grab his arm and pull him from the table. He relents. "Okay, I guess we're going upstairs."

In the lobby, I walk behind him like a prison guard. He continues talking; I continue not listening. I keep a smile on my face, sending out a message to all we pass: w*e are pleasant, we are professionals, the Director of Public Relations is not escorting the drunk, belligerent Director of Research up to his hotel room for a stern talking-to.* While smiling, I strategize. Steve has done his best to destroy this day—and possibly the entire statewide convention—but in public relations, there is a truth: you can spin anything. Every story is salvageable.

In the elevator, where we are alone, Steve stares at the floor and says, "You're angry with me."

"No. I'm not angry with you. You messed up, and I'm going to fix it, and then, when this has all been dealt with, I'm going to be mad at you."

"Okay. I'm sorry. That sounds like a fair deal."

I'm lying. I don't feel awful when, inside my hotel room, I push him a little too hard into the bathroom and he bangs his knee against the sink. Steve winces in pain. I strut past him, turn on the shower's cold water, and head back out.

"Take off your clothes," I tell him, "and get in the shower, and come out when you're less drunk."

"How will I know when I'm less drunk?"

I close the bathroom door.

I make the phone call on the balcony, where I can look out over Pittsburgh and feel the morning air and not want to walk back into the room and beat my friend's inebriated skull against the wall. The phone rings three times before Margo answers with a trepidatious "Hey."

I speak my piece in one breath:

"We're at the Holiday Inn and it's 8:30 in the morning and Steve is drunk and at 9:30 in the morning Steve will be presenting an hour-long speech to members of our

organization from across the state, and because Steve is drunk, and because I know
Steve well and because I know you well
and because I have a solid grasp on the
way your relationship works, I really, really need you to come here and help me fix
whatever is wrong with your boyfriend."

Margo says nothing.

I say, "Room 325, okay? Please."

I stand there, I smoke, and I wait.

#

When the door opens and Margo stands in
its wake, she becomes the most beautiful
woman to ever stand in a hotel doorway.

Margo's beauty is not something I've
dwelt on before. She's surely attractive,
with big eyes and a blond bob and thick
bangs, but I came to know her not as Margo, but as one-half of Margo & Steve. Their
relationship is a celebrity gossip magazine
at the supermarket checkout: I do not
question it, never have reason to read too

deep into it, and know only that it has always been there, a fixture.

She stands there, un-amused with a long coat covering her pajama pants, wearing red lipstick and slippers. Her existence is brilliant.

She says, "Where is he?"

I say, "Thank you, thank you, thank you so much."

She says, "Where is he?"

Margo opens the bathroom door, strolls in with her arms crossed, and stares down into the shower. I don't follow, but linger outside, looking in, unable to see what fate has befallen my Director of Research.

"Steve," she says, raising her voice to be heard over the running water. "Get out of the shower."

No response.

"Steve," she says, raising her voice for emphasis, "turn off the water."

No response.

She kicks off her slippers, shrugs off her jacket, and steps into the shower with her clothes on. This puts her out of my sight, but I picture the scene: Steve, crumpled on the floor with his head against the wall, and Margo, her clothes drenched, sitting next to him with her knees drawn to her chest, holding his hand and saying something.

The shower drowns out their words. I head back out onto the balcony. On my way, I snatch up the pad of Holiday Inn stationery upon which, while waiting for Margo's arrival, I had scrawled a list of options. Out above the city, another cigarette lit, I contemplate my written words: the Options, and the corresponding Reasons Why Not.

Postpone the presentation until later in the day.

No. The crowd will say, "That young PR guy, the one who looks like a college kid, he must have done something wrong, he has made a mess of this event."

Someone else could give the presentation.

No. Steve knows the data. Steve wrote the reports. Steve has spent hours upon hours readying himself.

I could give the presentation.

No one wants to see that. I know PR. I know how to schmooze. I know how to bullshit a press release. I know how to maintain relationships with unlikable but important business contacts. I don't know Steve's reports.

Steve could be semi-sobered.

He could put on his professional face and fake his way through an abbreviated version of the presentation. He could pull it off, provided Margo, wonderful Margo who has fished him out of a thousand spirals, can straighten out his mind.

My elbows sit on the railing, my body leaning forward, the pad in my hands dangling out over nothingness and the cigarette hanging from my mouth. When Margo appears to my right, soaking wet in her pajamas with her hair gone flat, she spooks the hell out of me. In fright, I clutch the railing with both hands. The notepad, let go, falls. My options plummet to the sidewalk five floors below.

I want to tell her, "That was fast," but she says, "Can I have a cigarette?"

She speaks the word *cigarette* clumsily, like a child speaking it for the first time. My mind stays on Steve and the fallen stationery as I pull the cigarettes from my pocket. I hold the open pack out to Margo. She grabs it. With one flick of her wrist, she tosses the whole thing over the railing.

I say, "Thanks for coming."

She says, "He doesn't really wanna talk to me."

"He does. He's just drunk and Steve. I don't know what's going on with him. He's never done this in the morning before, has he? And never at something like this. It's the statewide convention." I take the cigarette from my mouth and hold it between two fingers of the hand farthest from Margo. "His presentation's in twenty minutes. Thanks for coming, but I think we're destroyed."

Margo doesn't look at me. We both stare out at the city. She's drenched and shaking and the air's cold, but she hasn't put her coat or her slippers back on. It takes me longer than it should to drape my jacket over her shoulders.

She says, "I don't know if I'm gonna be much help. I think he's possibly really pissed at me."

"Why's that?"

She says, "Because I broke up with him."

Forty-five loud seconds tick by on my watch.

I ask, "Right now? In the shower?"

That's a stupid thing to say, the kind of stupid thing she would laugh at, but she doesn't laugh. "Last night." She scoots closer to the railing, still dripping, still shivering, and sticks her bare feet between the rail-bottoms. "I'm sorry. I should've waited. I didn't mean to wreck your whole thing."

The casualness with which Margo unloads this information upon me—*I'm so sorry for messing this up, Mike, guess I should've waited to end my relationship of five years, I wasn't really thinking*—leaves me without anything to say. I like Margo. I have nothing but good will toward the cold girl standing with me on the railing, but I picture Steve and feel the weight of a friend's responsibility: I should go to him, pull him out of the shower, and offer words of encouragement or comfort or vitriol. I can't come up with any of those words.

I can't solve the problem of Steve's presentation, much less the problem of his wounded relationship. I stay with Margo and she doesn't look at me.

"You broke up with him yesterday."

"Yeah. I guess so. I don't know. He didn't take it this hard last night."

"He didn't?"

"I mean, we kissed goodbye and stuff. Which I know isn't normal. But we were together for a long time and, oh, I'm sorry, I don't really wanna talk about this right now." She adds, quietly: "I really am sorry I can't help. But he isn't gonna talk to me. He just started yelling."

A pang in my stomach makes me feel like she's broken up with me. There can't be much time left to work with; I don't check my watch. Turning around and leaning back against the railing, facing the open sliding door and the empty hotel room, I see that Steve has not emerged. The shower has gone silent.

Margo turns, too, and we stare at an empty room. I can tell she wants to be anywhere but here. I'm indebted to her for even coming, but also I am an idiot, so I continue speaking.

"You got into the shower, though," I tell her. "To talk to him. To comfort him or whatever. Is that something you do after you break up with someone?"

"I don't know." Her voice doesn't come off as angry or annoyed; I believe she truly does not know. "It's not, like, really that simple, is it? I love Steve, you know. It's not like I just suddenly don't love him anymore."

"Then why did you break up with him?"

Margo says, "The same reason anyone breaks up with anyone. I didn't want to be with him anymore."

That doesn't make any sense. I push off the railing, walking back through the room, and she doesn't follow. I head into the bathroom and find Steve, still fully dressed, slumped into one corner of the shower. His head lolls against the wall. His eyes open just enough to see me.

"Really sorry, Mike," he tells me from the bottom. "This is a regret. This is gonna be a regret. I'm an asshole." He closes his eyes again. "Did she tell you about the bad thing?"

"Yeah," I tell him. "Steve."

"Mike?"

"You're not gonna be giving this presentation today, are you?'

He laughs. "*You're* the asshole," he says, and he keeps laughing.

I accept inevitability and check my watch. "I have no idea what I am going to do," I say. "You're on in fifteen minutes."

Steve smiles when he says, "You'll find a good spin to put on it." Before I can reply, he adds, "Since I'm too much of an asshole to present, can I sit alone in your shower a little longer and continue not dealing with my disasters?"

It's a difficult request to deny.

I gather up Margo's coat on my way out of the bathroom and find her standing by the hallway door, looking at me. She's heard everything. Instead of apologizing or comforting or saying something about not wanting to choose sides, I close the bathroom door behind me and hold out her coat, which she takes.

"Thanks," Margo says. Her eyes drift toward the door I've shut. "Is he alright? Is he gonna be okay?"

"He's sitting in my shower." I consider saying nothing more, but can't help myself from trying to improve the situation. "You can go back in and talk to him. He's not giving the presentation, and I have to go, but you can stay and talk to him. You can work it out, or whatever you need to do." She stares blank at me, not saying anything, so I keep saying things. "You said that you love him, and obviously he loves you, so you can go in there and talk about that."

That, I suppose, is when I notice how red her eyes have been this entire time. She stares right into mine.

"I know you're some kind of great PR guy, Mike, but this isn't, like, a press release. It's not something you can put a positive spin on. You can't make my relationship sound better to me than it is." She pauses. "Than it was." Her hand has already clutched the doorknob. "And plus, I have to be at work soon. I've gotta go to work. I'll get your jacket dry-cleaned."

"Yeah," I tell her. "Okay. I'll see you."

I probably won't. She opens the door and then she isn't in the room any longer.

I linger a few minutes more, despite being pressed for time, just to prevent any chance of running into Margo again between my room and the lobby. In these minutes, I sit on the edge of my bed and consider the morning ahead.

I will go downstairs, take my place at the podium, and try to find a positive spin.

My words, no matter how well-composed, will not change anything. The report will not be given. The company will live on. Margo will go to work and Steve will sit in my shower, and they will love each other, or they won't.

I will move on to a hotel lunch, where I will sit at a table alone, stare at a turkey sandwich, and convince myself I am a young professional.

ABOUT THE AUTHORS

Tomas Moniz edited *Rad Dad, Rad Families*, as well as the kids book *Collaboration/ Colaboración*. He's recently been published by *Barrelhouse* and *Longleaf Review*. In July 2019, he released a chapbook with Mason Jar Press, and his debut novel, *Big Familia*, on Acre Books, will be out in November. He has stuff on the internet but loves letters and pen pals: PO Box 3555, Berkeley CA 94703. He promises to write back.

Shannon McLeod is the author of the essay chapbook PATHETIC (Etchings Press). Her novella, WHIMSY, won the 2018 Wild Onion Novella Contest and is looking for a home for publication. Her writing has appeared in *Tin House Online*, *Necessary Fiction*, *Hobart*, *Joyland*, *Cheap Pop*, and

Wigleaf, among other publications. She teaches high school English in Virginia. You can find Shannon on twitter at @OcqueocSAM, or on her website, shannon-mcleod.com.

Maya White-Lurie's poetry has been published internationally, and she is a poetry reader for *Frontier Poetry* and *Sharkpack Annual*. She lives in Concepción, Chile, where she teaches English and tends her garden. Learn more at her website: mayawhitelurie.wordpress.com.

Scott Garson is the author of IS THAT YOU, JOHN WAYNE?—a collection of stories. He teaches in the English Department at the University of Missouri.

Wandeka Gayle is a Jamaican writer, visual artist, and Assistant Professor of Creative Writing at Spelman College. She has received fellowships from Kimbilio Fiction, the Hurston/Wright Foundation, the Callaloo Creative Writing Workshop, and the Martha's Vineyard Institute of Creative Writing. Gayle has a PhD in English/Creative Writing from the University of Louisiana at Lafayette. Her writing has appeared or is forthcoming in *Transition*, *The Rumpus*, *Interviewing the Caribbean*, and other journals. Her collection of short stories, *Motherland and Other Stories*, is forthcoming by Peepal Tree Press in July 2020.

Noah Cain teaches high school English, coaches hockey, and writes in Winnipeg, Canada. His writing has appeared or is forthcoming in a variety of publications including *CV2*, *Prairie Fire*, and *Glass: A Journal of Poetry*.

Derek Heckman was born in Peoria, IL, and holds an MFA in fiction from the University of Montana. His stories have been published in *The Collapsar*, *Wigleaf*, *Ellipsis Zine*, and *The Furious Gazelle*. The start of his novel "A Beginner's Guide to Coming Back from the Dead" was featured in the inaugural issue of *Embark Journal*. He currently lives in Boston, Massachusetts.

Carman C. Curton has been published in *Corvid Queen* and *Snakeskin Poetry Magazine* and was a finalist in the Fiction War Fall 2018 contest. Carman consumes caffeine while writing a series of micro-stories called QuickFics, which she leaves in random places for people to find. You can find her on Twitter @CarmanCCurton.

James Tate Hill is the author of *Academy Gothic* (Southeast Missouri State University Press, 2015), winner of the Nilsen Prize for a First Novel. His fiction and nonfiction have appeared or are forthcoming in *Literary Hub*, *Prairie Schooner*, *Writer's Digest*, *Story Quarterly*, and *Waxwing*, among others. He serves as fiction editor for the literary journal *Monkeybicycle* and writes a monthly audio books column for *Lit Hub*. A native of West Virginia, he lives in Greensboro, North Carolina, with his wife.

Chloe Yelena Miller lives in Washington, D.C., with her husband, child and their many books. Her poetry chapbook *Unrest* was published by Finishing Line Press. Her work has appeared in *Alimentum, The Cortland Review, McSweeney's, Narrative Magazine, Poet's Market,* and *Storyscape Literary Journal,* among others. The poems published here come from a manuscript of poems about miscarriage, pregnancy, and early motherhood.

Chloe teaches writing at the University of Maryland University College and Politics & Prose Bookstore, as well as privately. chloeyelenamiller.com

@ChloeYMiller

Siân Griffiths lives in Ogden, Utah, where she directs the graduate program in English at Weber State University. Her writing has been published in *The Georgia Review, Prairie Schooner, The Cincinnati Review, American Short Fiction, Indiana Review,* and *The Rumpus,* among other publications. Her debut novel, *Borrowed Horses* (New Rivers Press), was a semi-finalist for the 2014 VCU Cabell First Novelist Award. Currently, she reads fiction as part of the editorial team at *Barrelhouse*. For more information, visit sbgriffiths.com.

Clarence Barbee has been teaching in the greater Denver area for four years. He enjoys the challenge of children, the mentally ill, and finding peace, but not administrators. Writing has over-taken his passion of performing on stages currently. He's a dad over 21 two times over, he is known on Twitter as @former402poet.

Jonathan Persinger is a teacher, writer, and alleged young professional. He was born and raised in Pennsylvania, and now teaches high school English in the Northern Neck of Virginia. His work has appeared in *Cracked*, *The Potomac Review*, and *Scribble*, among others. Learn more at jonathanpersinger.wordpress.com.

Acknowledgments

Many thanks to the authors for trusting us with your work, to Sheila Salaneck for helping us select poetry, to DeMisty D. Bellinger for assistance with selecting pieces and editing the book, to Stuart Buck for creating the excellent cover, and to Mythic Picnic for coming up with the idea for this anthology and providing energy and funding to help create it.

And of course many, many thanks to readers of this book. Please share it with your friends and family, rate it, recommend it, take a picture of yourself with it, order it from your local library. We are a very small press publishing mostly under-the-radar writers, and anything you do to spread the word is a big help and greatly appreciated.

Most of all, thank you to all of our teachers. Whether you work in pre-K, K-12, or higher ed, we stand with you.

More titles from Malarkey Books

Dear Writer: Stories That Just Weren't a Good Fit at the Time, an anthology of frequently rejected fiction, edited by Alan Good and Jason Gong

Forest of Borders by Nicholas Grider

Visitor by Craig Rodgers

The Life of the Party Is Harder to Find by Adrian Sobol

There's also plenty to read on our website, malarkeybooks.com.

Printed in the USA
CPSIA information can be obtained
at www.ICGtesting.com
LVHW010423021223
765527LV00025B/88